Five Mile, an imprint of
Bonnier Publishing Australia
Level 6, 534 Church Street, Richmond, Victoria 3121
www.fivemile.com.au

ISBN 978 1 76040 768 1

Printed in China 5 4 3 2 1

Rory's Story

The Five Mile Press

Rory is having a terrible time!
He has a new baby sister.
She is too small to play with and she cries a lot,
waving her little, clenched paws in the air.
Even worse, his mother and father are always busy.

'Will you cuddle me?' asks Rory.
'In a minute,' says Mother.
'First I have to feed the baby.'
Rory waits …
'Will you cuddle me now?' asks Rory.
'Soon,' says Mother.
'First I have to wash the baby's ears.'
Rory waits …

'Will you give me a ride on your back?' asks Rory.
'Soon,' says Mother.
'First I have to wash the baby's face.'
Rory waits …
'Will you give me a ride now?' asks Rory.
'Soon,' says Mother.
'First I have to wash the baby's tail.'
Rory sighs and goes to see if his father
will play with him.

'Will you climb a tree with me?' Rory asks Father.
'Soon,' says Father.
'First I have to finish tidying the den for the baby.'
Rory waits …

'Will you climb a tree now?' asks Rory.
'Soon,' says Father.
'First I have to teach the baby how to growl.
Do you want to help?'
'No,' says Rory, feeling a bit left out and sad and bored.
Everyone is so busy.

Rory goes outside and sees
Hippo bouncing along the path.
'Hi!' says Hippo. 'Shall we play a game?'
'Okay,' says Rory, grinning.
'What shall we play?'

'Crocodiles!'

First Hippo pretends
to be a crocodile chasing Rory.

Then Rory pretends
to be a crocodile chasing Hippo.

The two friends run in circles until they fall over,
laughing and kicking their legs in the air.
They pretend to SNAP! big crocodile teeth.
SNIP SNAP! Growwwl!

Mother opens the door, looking angry.
'Ssshh, you two!' she says.
'You are making so much noise
that you've woken the baby.'

Mother goes back inside.
Rory and Hippo can hear
the little cub crying, but after
a while the sound stops.

'Let's take a look,' says Hippo,
'I haven't seen your new baby sister yet.'
So they tiptoe inside.
Mother is holding the baby
and singing softly to her.

'Hush little tiger, don't growl and cry,
Mama's going to sing you a lullaby.
The jungle is green, the sky is blue,
Your brother Rory wants to cuddle you.'

'I don't know how!' says Rory.
'It's easy,' says Mother.
'Sit down and I'll show you.'
Mother brings the baby over to Rory.
Suddenly, Rory's new baby sister is
all cuddled up on his lap.
She feels warm and soft. She smiles.
Rory can't help smiling back.

'You're nice,' says Rory.
His baby sister makes a gurgly growl back.
She clasps his paw tight.
Then she closes her eyes and falls asleep.

Rory and Hippo creep back outside
to play a quiet game.
'She's cute,' says Hippo.
'You're lucky, Rory.'
'Yes,' says Rory. 'I am.'

Now Rory tells everyone in the jungle
about his new baby sister.
Then he practises his own lullaby
to sing to her.

'Hush little sister, don't cry at all,
Rory will hold you so you won't fall.
The jungle is green, the sky is blue,
Your brother Rory is proud of you.'